HOW THE *Sea* BEGAN

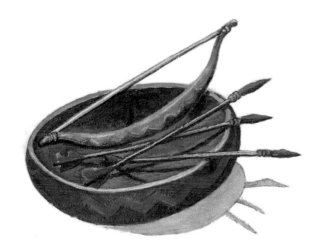

This book is dedicated to my wife Mercy,
and to my daughter Mercy Christine,
and to my son Ivan.
With special thanks to my compadre
Robert Casilla.

Clarion Books
a Houghton Mifflin Company imprint
215 Park Avenue South, New York, NY 10003
Text and Illustrations copyright © 1993 by George Crespo

Book designed by Sylvia Frezzolini
Printed in the USA

Library of Congress Cataloging-in-Publication Data

Crespo, George.
   How the sea began : a Taino myth / retold and illustrated by
George Crespo.
      p.   cm.
   Retelling of a story collected by Father Ramón Pané.
   Summary: The gourd containing the bow and arrow of the great
departed hunter Yayael produces a torrent of water that becomes the
world's ocean.
   ISBN 0-395-63033-9
   1. Taino Indians—Legends.   [1. Taino Indians—Legends.   2. Indians
of the West Indies—Legends.   3. Ocean—Folklore.]   I. Pané, Ramón,
d. 1571.   II. Title.
F1619.2.T3C74   1993
398.2'09729—dc20
[E]   91-39651
                                             CIP
                                             AC

HOR   10   9   8   7   6   5   4   3   2   1

HOW THE *Sea* BEGAN

A TAINO MYTH RETOLD AND ILLUSTRATED BY

George Crespo

Clarion Books · *New York*

In the beginning of time, before the land was surrounded by sea, in a place called Zuania, there were four great mountains. One mountain was called Boriquén, Land of Brave Men. And on that mountain, in the village of Coabey, lived an old man named Yaya with his wife, Itiba, and their only son, Yayael. Yayael was a skilled hunter.

Yayael hunted with a bow that his father had carved for him out of tabonuco wood. It is said that the tabonuco tree is the home of spirits, and that its wood holds magical powers.

This saying may be true, because when Yayael went out hunting he always brought back game. The people of Coabey ate well, even when the other hunters came back empty-handed.

One day while Yayael was out hunting he saw that the sky was darkening in the east. A flock of swallows flying before the lowering clouds circled around his head, flapping and beating their wings. Yayael knew this was a warning that Guabancex, the terrible goddess of hurricanes, was coming. He quickly hid his bow and arrows under a large rock and ran toward the village, hoping to reach safety before the winds overtook him.

Guabancex created a hurricane that struck with tremendous force. The winds howled and raged for hours. The villagers who had been working in their fields sought shelter in a cave nearby. Yaya and Itiba prayed to the supreme god Yúcahu that Yayael would come through the storm unharmed.

When the winds died down, the people thanked Yúcahu, then ventured from the cave. They found that their huts had been flattened by the storm. Yaya and Itiba waited, but Yayael did not appear.

Yaya went to search for his son. He found the bow and arrows where Yayael had hidden them, but of Yayael himself there was no sign.

When Itiba saw her husband returning with their son's bow and arrows in his hands, she called out Yayael's name. Then she fell down weeping at her husband's feet.

Yaya reverently placed Yayael's bow and arrows in a large gourd. Then he sat down beside his wife and wept too.

The villagers helped one another rebuild their homes. When the time for grieving was over, they helped Yaya and Itiba hang the gourd from the ceiling of their hut, where the bow and arrows would be safe, just in case Yayael's spirit should wish to visit them. Yaya picked up his own bow and arrows and went to hunt, for now the village could no longer depend on Yayael to bring home meat.

Though the men of the village hunted every day, they seldom brought home enough for everyone. All were hungry. Even the children, who were always fed first, were becoming thin and sickly.

One evening Yaya asked Itiba to lower the gourd that held Yayael's weapons. "I want to see our son's bow," he said. "Perhaps it still holds the power of the tabonuco."

As Itiba lowered the gourd to the floor, it tipped just a little. Out spilled many beautiful, plump fish. Yaya and Itiba were astonished. They had never before seen such fish—large and silvery and still breathing, as if freshly taken from the water. Itiba cooked them and invited the whole village to share the meal.

The villagers rejoiced in their good fortune. They sang, "Baharí Yayael"—We honor you, Yayael—and went to bed with full stomachs.

The following day, all the villagers went out to work in the
fields. They left four boys to guard the gourd that held Yayael's
bow and arrows, the bow and arrows that turned into fish.

The boys were curious and hungry. The higher the sun climbed into the sky, the more curious and hungry they became. One boy stood up on tiptoe and tried to peer into the gourd. Then a second boy tried to climb up and see inside. They were joined by the other two, and together they brought the gourd down to the floor.
Out flopped four fish, just the right size for four hungry boys.

The boys cooked the fish and ate them. Then they ate four more. They sang praises to Yayael's spirit and lowered the gourd again for more fish.

Suddenly the boys heard Yaya and the villagers returning from the fields. Afraid of being caught, they hurried to raise the gourd to the ceiling.

In their haste, they failed to secure the rope that held the gourd in its place. The gourd fell to the ground and broke open.

Water rushed out of the broken gourd. In an instant everything in the hut was afloat. A wave swept the boys out of the hut and out of the village and left them, choking and sputtering, on the path that led to the fields. There Yaya and the other villagers found them; the water tasted of salt, the boys said, like the salt of tears.

Water continued to flow from the gourd. It flowed and rose to cover the land. And fish swam out of the gourd—large fish and small fish, starfish, urchins, and jellyfish, all kinds of sea creatures came out of the gourd to fill the water with life.

The villagers gathered on the mountaintop and watched as the waters covered Zuania. When at last the water stopped rising, they saw that their mountain, Boriquén, was now an island. They gave their thanks to Yúcahu, dressed themselves festively, and celebrated with music and dancing, because as long as there were fish in the sea, they would not go hungry.

And this is one story of how the sea began.

How the Sea Began is a Taíno creation myth. The Taíno, whose name meant "the good ones," were an Arawak people of the Orinoco Basin in South America who migrated to the Greater Antilles around the year 1000. Zuania, where the story opens, was the Taíno name for the South American mainland, the Taíno place of origin. The island of Boriquén is now known as Puerto Rico; the other three mountains referred to in the story became Cuba, Jamaica, and the Dominican Republic/Haiti.

The Taíno were animists who believed that the natural world was inhabited by a variety of spirits. They worshipped a supreme deity, Yúcahu, and many lesser gods or *cemís*, one of whom was Guabancex.

It was the custom among the Taíno to keep the bones of dead relatives in a gourd hung from the ceiling of the hut. When Yaya places Yayael's weapons in the gourd, he is symbolically burying his son.

How the Sea Began was collected in its original form by Fray Ramón Pané in Hispañola, now the Dominican Republic, nearly five hundred years ago. Admiral Christopher Columbus commissioned Pané to record the beliefs and customs of the Taíno people. Pané's work *Relación acerca de las antigüedades de los indios* is the only existing document on Taíno mythology and was the first ethnological study done in the New World.

Pronunciation Guide					
Zuania	soo AH nya	Itiba	EE tee bah	Guabancex	gwah bahn SEKS
Boriquén	bo ri KEN	Yayael	ah yah EL	Yúcahu	YOO kah hoo
Coabey	kwah BAY	tabonuco	tah bo NOO ko	Baharí	bah hah REE
Ya Ya	JIA yah				